TOO MANY MEN
ON THE ICE

Steven O'Connor

Copyright © 2022 Steven O'Connor
All rights reserved
First Edition

PAGE PUBLISHING
Conneaut Lake, PA

First originally published by Page Publishing 2022

ISBN 978-1-6624-2940-8 (pbk)
ISBN 978-1-6624-2941-5 (digital)

Printed in the United States of America

In March 1979, I was hired by the Bristol Bay Health Corporation in Dillingham, Alaska to teach swimming to the native people in the Bristol Bay area. The villages in the Bristol Bay area relied on fishing for their livelihood. Several drownings over the past few years had brought about the job opportunity. Four years of life guarding in the cold Atlantic at Salisbury Beach, Massachusetts, plus my water safety instructor certification (WSI), made me qualified. I was out of my mind with anticipation. My mom and dad wanted me to fly to Alaska. My little brother and sister want me to hitch. I had a plan all my own.

My cousin Dan, a year older than me, had graduated from Colgate University the previous year and was working for Notinis (a food delivery service in Lowell, Massachusetts) before taking the plunge into the rat race that a Colgate degree demanded. He was the big brother: smart, funny, athletic, and fearless. He was the life of every party he attended. He could pull off the rare double of being the loudest guy at the party, as well as the funniest. Dee, our grandfather, called him loquacious. I was his caddy/bodyguard. Dan always did the talking—with the ladies, the ticket scalpers, and the bouncers. He would always try to BS rather than pay a cover. Any angle in, Dan would take it.

By the time I was twenty-one, he had saved me thousands of dollars because of his ability to convince (or connive). When we went to out of town games or concerts, he would invent a crisis at the gate in order to circumvent the cost of tickets. His favorite was tickets lost by airlines. He would work himself into such an emotional state that dozens of kindhearted, gullible gatekeepers would let him slide, taking me, and whoever else was with us, in for free.

Dan was especially good at reading the emotions of the room, be it a bar, a party, or an NHL arena. This behavior would sometimes lead to physical confrontations when Dan pushed too far. He would persist until he knew when to stop, then quickly go with Plan B. On these occasions we would just run for the hills; every man for himself, reconnoiter later. We were way better runners than we were fighters. That he never went out for drama club while in school was a giant waste. We were more like brothers than cousins.

Our dads were brothers, born three years apart. They were inseparable. They were also maniacs, and we were the ones who benefited. When my Uncle Bucky took us up Mount Monadnock, his brother Gerry would take us up Mount Washington. When Gerry scored World Series tickets to the Red Sox vs Cardinals, Bucky got us in to watch a US Olympic Hockey team practice. By them trying to outdo the other, our lives were incredibly enriched. Needless to say, they were great dads. By the time we were twelve, our dads had inspired/brainwashed us to the point that Dan was giving Churchill speeches and I was reciting Robert Service poems to our siblings and our parents' friends, for whom we loved performing.

One great one-upsmanship that Bucky and Gerry engaged in was also very beneficial to us—one that opened up other doors of interests. Bucky gave me the *Baseball Encyclopedia* for my birthday one year, so a month later, Gerry gave Dan the *Hockey Encyclopedia* for his birthday. These gifts actually caused our parents to have us tested for OCD (obsessive-compulsive disorder). You see, the encyclopedias put us over the edge because it was the combination of two of our biggest interests: sports and geography. Fortunately, we scored low on the Brown-Yale Obsessive Compulsive Scale, and our parents gave us our books back. Newly empowered, we seized on their guilt and requested a ride into Boston so we could purchase a better map of Canada, to better see our favorite places: Flin Flon, Manitoba, and the Northwest Territories. We had a new obsession—Arctic explorers: Alexander Mackenzie was my guy, and Amundsen was Dan's.

Another great thing for us was that our moms got along, so every Saturday night of our young lives, we would get dropped off at Manor Circle, our grandparent's house. Going there was like going from the fire into the frying pan. Dee, our grandfather, was one in a billion. He quit school at thirteen to work in a bank and became the Deputy Commissioner of Banks for the state of Massachusetts. He knew everybody. When he would take Dan and me to the Celts or Bruins' games, we would have a contest to see how many people Dee would converse with. Depending on where he took us, the total could be over one hundred.

Dee had two things that took precedence over everything: Notre Dame Football and Boston Bruins hockey. Dee was a subway alum of Notre Dame, and on his honeymoon, he took his new bride to a Notre Dame-Army football game. My grandmother knew then, get with the program or stay home. As a result, my Nana was just as bad. One time in Boston, she recognized Leon Hart of Heisman Trophy fame and told the famous football player all about our peewee football team.

Every Saturday in the fall, the schedule would revolve around kickoff. Often it would become a double header when the Bruins dropped the puck. Dee had met No. 15, Milt Schmidt, when he worked for the bank and became his friend. We had met Mr. Schmidt once, and it was a very special moment for us. Milt Schmidt was from Kitchener, Ontario, and made his first appearance in a Bruin's uniform in 1937. Schmidt and his boyhood friends, Woody Dumart and Bobby Bauer, formed one of the greatest lines in NHL history—the Kraut Line. They brought home the Stanley Cup in '39 and '41, but World War II interrupted their run. Ten years later, Schmidt won the Hart Trophy as MVP, but no more cups, symbolic of the National Hockey League's supremacy, came Boston's way. He retired in '55 after amassing 575 points, to become head coach, then general manager.

Notre Dame always did well, but the Bruins had fallen on hard times. They made the finals in '58 and '59, but had not made the post season for all of the 1960s. In those years, you could say Detroit was our number two. Bucky had met Gordie Howe in 1951 and was so impressed with him that he jumped ship. He became a Red Wings fan. This did not go over well with Dee, but he respected Bucky's motives. How can you argue against Gordie Howe? The Red Wings were worse than the Bruins in the '60s, so I jumped that ship to the Toronto Maple Leafs. I had seen them play a few times, and I liked Dave Keon. When they won the Cup in '67, I was glad, but I would give anything to have the Bruins in the mix of the best teams.

There was not a lot to be hopeful about, until October 1966, when Bobby Orr from Parry Sound, Ontario, stepped onto the Garden ice. We were there that night against the Red Wings. Howe scored a goal and ran Orr every chance he could, but he also saw the future that night, and it was good for us. We even got Bucky to admit that the Bruins would win the Cup before Detroit. By Orr's second year, the team had improved twenty wins and when Mr. Schmidt traded Pit Martin and friends to the Black Hawks for Phil Esposito, Ken Hodge, and Fred Stanfield, we were on our way.

The 69–70 team was magic. By January, the league knew that Boston would contend for the Cup. The Bruins took out the Rangers in six, then the Blackhawks in four in the playoffs. The St. Louis Blues had beaten the Penguins in the semifinals, setting up a Boston-St. Louis final. The Bruins dominated the first three games, and Dee had a party on Sunday, May 10, for game four. St. Louis almost wrecked the party when they scored late to send the game into OT. But Orr of Parry Sound, and Sanderson of Niagara Falls, ended it quickly.

"Sanderson to Orr…and Bobby Orr scores! And the Boston Bruins have won the Stanley Cup!" Thank you, Dan Kelly.

I will never get sick of watching that. Manor Circle went wild! Three generations of hockey fans jumping up and down screaming! What a moment! The 1970s were looking good for us.

*****

We were all assembled back at Manor Circle on April 9 for Dee's seventy-fifth birthday party, when my "Dan Plan" went into motion. Everyone was in good spirits; the Bruins were rolling to another showdown with Montreal, and I was excited about going north. I cornered Dan and began reminiscing about all the great road trips we'd had over the years, and how it was sad that those days were done for him now that he was a college graduate. Too bad. But if we tuned up Dan's car, "Eddie," took all our savings, camped out off-road, we could make the ultimate road trip: 5,000 miles across Canada to Alaska.

We could start in Montreal, go to an Expos game, then head west. We could go to Flin Flon, the Northwest Territories, and walk in the footsteps of Alexander Mackenzie. We could go to Saskatoon to see where Howe grew up, maybe even Parry Sound. When he told me that he'd talk to his folks and think about it, I knew my plan had worked.

The next day he drove to my house with a maple leaf taped on his forehead, stood on Ed, and belted the first verse of "Oh Canada." I let out a howl.

Since I had to be in Dillingham, Alaska, by May 12, we figured we could leave at the end of April and that would give us plenty of time to cross the continent. However, other events would dictate our entire trip: Bruins vs Canadiens Stanley Cup semifinals.

The 1970 team was so talented we all assumed that we were on the cusp of one of the great dynasties of all time. But something happened in '71; his name was Ken Dryden, and he would haunt us for a decade. He was called up with six games remaining in the '71 season as a rookie, and all he did was win the Conn Smythe as the NHL Playoff MVP.

In game seven of the quarter finals, the Bruins rained forty-eight shots on him. He stopped forty-six. We hated him. He was tall, quick, and brilliant, and he was the best goalie in the world. Montreal ended our Cup run at one.

We got it back in '72 when we beat the Rangers in six, but New York, behind Eddie Giacomin, got their revenge the next year, beating us in five in the quarters. New York then got pummeled by the Black Hawks in the semis, who then became road kill in the finals by Montreal.

In '74 we were back in the finals, only to be stoned by Conn Smythe winner, Bernie Parent, and the Flyers. In '75, the year Orr scored forty-six goals and won his last Norris trophy as the NHL's best defenseman, the Bruins got bounced in the measly preliminary round by the Chicago Blackhawks. We won game one by a score of 8-2, but Tony Esposito was immense, and they closed us out in three. Bobby Orr would never win another playoff game, his career effectively over at age twenty-seven because of knee injuries.

In '76 Orr and Espo were gone, but we made the semis with our new stars, Jean Ratelle and Brad Park, whom we got from the Rangers when we traded Esposito. Bernie Parent was once again our Cup killer. The defeat had earned the Flyers the right to be humiliated 4-0 in the finals by Montreal, a team that was on its way to being called one of the best of all time.

In 1977, we had to watch Guy LaFleur skate around the Boston Garden holding his Conn Symthe, and the Canadiens hoisting their second Cup in a row after they spanked us 4-0 in the finals. What was worse was 1978. We made the finals, but lost a heartbreaking game two in the Forum when who else but Guy Lafleur beat Bruin's goalie Gerry Cheevers in overtime.

Game four was literally a bloodbath. Stan Jonathan, no. 17, pummeled Montreal tough guy, Pierre Bouchard, into the hospital, and we won the game but lost the series in six. Once again, we had to endure the agony of watching them skate around the Boston Garden ice holding the Stanley Cup high above their smug heads. How sweet it must have been for their arrogant selves. They had finished an amazing three-year Cup run, going 36-6 in the playoffs.

Nineteen-seventy-nine was a new season. The Bruins won the Adams Division with forty-three wins while Montreal took the Norris Division with fifty-two. We had a deep team, a tough team, led by our crazy coach, Don Cherry. We knew we could dethrone those pompous champs. We had Park, Ratelle, Cashman, Middleton, Marcotte, Schmautz, McNab, O'Reilly, with Cheevers and Gilbert in net. We also had Stan Jonathan, who was a Tasmanian Devil on skates. The chaos he inflicted was often gut-wrenchingly funny. He was a wild card that could win a game on pure will. He had replaced Sanderson as Dan's favorite player.

We also had two home-grown guys from Massachusetts: Mike Milbury from Walpole and Bobby Miller from Billerica. We would go to the Chelmsford Forum and watch Miller and his Billerica buddies dominate any team that stood in their way. By his sophomore year in high school, it was obvious that he was the real thing. He caused a buzz every time he stepped on the ice. The Bruins got him after a great career at UNH and the US Olympic team, but not before Bobby caused an international incident when he had to take care of some local Austrian punks. He was a born Bruin.

By mid-April, it was obvious that it would happen all over again. The semifinals would be the real finals because these were the two best teams in the league. The Canadiens, coached by Scotty Bowman, were truly a great team. They were the perfect storm of offense, defense, and goal tending. They had the league's best goalie in Dryden, the best defenseman in Larry Robinson, the best right wing in Lafluer, and the best defensive forward in Bob Gainey. Throw in Houle, Lapointe, Sevard, Tremblay, Lambert, Shutt, and Mondou, and you had a team without a weakness. It was shaping up to be a classic series.

The puck would drop for game one on Thursday, April 26. We now had our traveling agenda. Dan checked an Expos schedule, and they were in town as well. Things were really taking shape.

Our car was a black 1970 Ford Falcon, two-door that answered to the name Falcon Eddy, or Ed for short. He was dependable, okay on gas, despite the V-8 he was packing, and roomy enough to sleep in. He had a kick-ass 8-track system and a good radio. He was part of the family. That Dan intended to sell him to a dealer in Anchorage was never even talked about.

Our front-seat possessions had to be clutter resistant, so we made some rules. Must-takes were, of course, our new Rand-McNally that answered to Randy, our *Hockey Encyclopedia* that we called Milt (for Mr. Schmidt), a Canadian Almanac with all relevant history and geography facts, he was Cal. We had an 8-track case that held ten tapes, so that would be a tough cut, one that we actually had a meeting for. We also packed our Bruins jerseys. I took no. 4, Orr, and no. 10, Ratelle. Dan took no. 16, Sanderson, and no. 17, Jonathan. Dan also brought a family treasure: a mint condition no. 9 Detroit Red Wings that Bucky had given him with instructions to wear only in Saskatchewan.

STEVEN O'CONNOR

On the morning of April 25, we control-cracked a Molson with Ed's lug wrench and pulled out of Manor Circle, heading north through Lebanon, New Hampshire, and Burlington, Vermont. We were staying with a family friend in St. Albans, Vermont, that night. The next morning, we hit the Canadian border, said a small prayer at Customs, and said goodbye to the USA. Hopefully, the next time we entered our country, it would be in the state of Alaska.

QUEBEC

Facts

527,079 square miles
Highest point: Mount D'Iberville 5417'
Location: 1,000 miles northeast of Montreal
Canada's largest province and the only one with land over 60*
    north latitude
(All other land over 60⁰ are territories.)

Quick History

Jacques Cartier was the Columbus of Canada. He landed on the Gaspé Peninsula and got as far as present-day Montreal in 1535. Seventy years later, Samuel Champlain was next up, but he failed in his attempt to establish a fur trading post and was repelled by the indigenous Mohawks. Regardless, the French were here to stay. Different flags flew over Quebec during the tumultuous 1770s after the epic Battle of the Plains of Abraham in 1774. The flag said Britain, but the culture said France. It's been an interesting marriage ever since, but both sides are Canadian first and foremost.

Hockey Opines

All-time team: Maurice Richard, Jean Beliveau, Guy Lafleur, Doug Harvey, Serge Savard, Jacques Plante
Toughest omission: Yvan Cournoyer and Jean Ratelle
Also: Buddy O'Connor (just because).

Notable

Quebec has twenty-four native sons in the Hockey Hall of Fame.

We were introduced to Montreal as kids, and we kept that relationship going as soon as Dan got his driver's license. We would make the five-hour trip a few times every year, either for an Expos game or a Bruins-Canadiens game. By then we knew where the good values were with hotels, so we'd either get a room or crash in one of Montreal's many beautiful parks, Rutherford Parc being my personal favorite. Every so often, these circumstances would lead to a meeting with the RCMP. One time a Dudley (our code name for an officer) saw us emerging from the bushes of Rutherford and had us totally convinced that we had to pay a $100 membership fee to National Parks of Canada for the sleep we had just taken. The officer had us sweating panic until he pulled the plug on his prank. He liked that we were sports fans, adding to the economy, albeit in a small way. He probably was also happy because the previous night his team had vanquished our team 6-2.

We found a room in the Crescent District for $34 and made our way to Jarry Park. The San Diego Padres were in town, and we had never seen Ozzie Smith, Dave Winfield, or Rollie Fingers play. We got two tickets and two beers for under $10 and watched Gary Carter and his buds put a beating on the visitors. Before the game, we forced our way into a conversation with ex-Red Sox player Bill Lee. We told him in the autograph line that Stan Papi sucked and that we miss him. He told us to tell Leo at the Cask'n Flagon to have a cold one ready for him in October after the Expos beat the Red Sox in the World Series. We were sad that he wasn't pitching. It definitely affected our level of enthusiasm. Bad move Haywood Sullivan. After the game we walked around town conserving our money and feeling the anticipation of tomorrow's game one semifinal.

After checking out the next day, we had coffee and doughnuts and made our way downtown, leaving Ed safe in a lot. He was a little out of place with all the French cars surrounding him, but Ed was very adaptable. We made the decision to go all in wearing our jerseys, knowing full well that we would have to be on our toes at all times with those targets on our backs. I put on my no. 10 Jean Ratelle, and Dan decided to go with no. 17 Stan Jonathan, much scarier. We hoped we didn't run into any of Pierre Bouchard's friends. The fight from last year was still fresh, even though Bouchard was no longer a Canadien.

We scrambled the pregame around Cabot Square until we saw the front entrance of the Forum. The Holy Cathedral. The epicenter of the hockey world. There it was in front of us. We had made it inside five times and had never seen the Bruins win.

The Forum was built in 1924 and home to more Stanley Cups (twenty-one) than anywhere in the world. Only once in the history of the building did a visiting team skate the Cup around the Forum ice. The 1928 Rangers—we had missed that series. We knew getting inside would set our budget way back, so we headed back to the Crescent and to the next best thing: Winston Churchill's. We had spent some enjoyable nights in Winston's over the years when we came up for Bruin games. We'd always stop there the night before to chat up the many Bruins who would be spending the night on the town. One night we got into a discussion with Bruin tough guy John Wensink. We got him going when we asked him if any of the Minnesota North Stars had ever said boo to him after he challenged the entire bench to a fight in '77. He had not heard from any. Going into such hostile territory dressed as we were required some preparation: knowledge.

That we could rattle off Cup winners, Conn Smythe winners, Norris winners, and Lady Byngers gave us the confidence to penetrate the enemy. As long as we genuflected on our way in and out, maintained civil discourse, and didn't overserve ourselves with Molson Blues, we would be fine. This was not our first rodeo.

Wearing no. 10 was easy duty. Jean Ratelle was coming off his fourth season as a Bruin since the trade that brought him and Brad Park to the Bruins for Esposito. Ratelle was a total class act; he usually popped in about thirty goals with his soft hands and keen mind. He was also a Masterson Trophy winner, and in our family, the name Masterson was said in the company of Lou Gehrig and Ernie

Davis. My Uncle Bucky had seen Masterson play college hockey and thought he was the total package of talent, brains and humility.

Bill Masterson was a kid from Winnipeg who went to the University of Denver, leading them to an NCAA Championship in 1961. Upon graduating with a degree in electrical engineering, Masterson was drafted by the Canadiens but never got even a cup of coffee. He retired from hockey, got his master's degree, and went to work on the Apollo Space Program. When the NHL expanded in 1967, it gave Masterson the chance to fulfill a lifelong goal and play in the NHL. In November of 1967, he scored the first goal in the history of the Minnesota North Stars. On January 13, 1968, just three months into the season, Masterson was killed in an on-ice collision in a game against the California Golden Seals. He was twenty-nine. The Masterson Trophy was soon established. It is awarded to a player who best exemplifies the qualities of perseverance, sportsmanship, and dedication to ice hockey that Masterson displayed. His number, 19, still hangs in the rafters of the Met Center in Bloomington, Minnesota. The name Masterton is bulletproof in any hockey argument.

That night, I dared anybody to say anything bad about Ratelle. I kept my Masterson card in my pocket, but I did get a few smiles from the enemy when I responded "Lac-Saint Jean" to the cat calls I got about my Bruins jersey.

Winston's was jam packed on that Thursday night, and it was 98 percent–2 percent Canadiens, judging by the jerseys. We met some fellow Bruin fans from Niagara Falls, Ontario, home of two great Bruin characters: Derek Sanderson and Terry O'Reilly. O'Reilly was on the '79 team and was pure energy—not a great skater but as tough as anyone on the ice. The guys from Niagara Falls said they were buds with no. 24, so we stayed close to them.

The game was closely checked, and good chances did not come in the first ten minutes. At 13:52, Jacques Lemaire beat Cheevers, and Montreal was on the board first. The second period was all Bruins. First Ratelle on a power play from Middleton and Park at 3:37, then Donny Marcotte from O'Reilly at 5:34 put us up 2-1. We were suddenly aware that as the second period ticked away we were becoming less popular.

Between periods, I tried a conversation with a brown-haired, blue-eyed French beauty, but my C- ninth-grade French got me nowhere. You were right, Mrs. Vigneaux, I should have done my homework. I now know that.

Dan looked my way just as the puck dropped for the third period and said, "Do you think we can do this? And if we do, we are out the door the second the horn sounds."

The twist of nerves had gone from my stomach to my shoulders, but I thought we could steal it. It took less than four minutes for Lefleur to tie the score. A feeling of resignation soon turned overwhelming. We knew it was just a matter of time. Like I said, this was not our first rodeo.

Pierre Larouche ended the suspense at 12:17, and Doug Jarvis empty-netted us into the night. It was there for us; we let it slip away. You rarely get a chance to win in that building. I hoped we'd get another chance. We burned deep down inside, but we played nice in the sandbox with our new friends who now liked us again.

We walked to Ed, focusing on the bright spots, not yet grasping that we were about to begin our journey across the continent. If we could get a few hours on the road we'd feel better about the day. I took the first shift since I had milked two beers for the entire game. Dan, who could fall asleep on a picket fence, climbed into the back. I turned west on Route 17 and let the sweet sounds of the Marshall Tucker Band begin our journey west.

The Trans-Canada Highway is almost five thousand miles long, going from Newfoundland to British Columbia. You have to take a ferry from Newfoundland to Nova Scotia, but once you get on the ground there, you can drive straight to the Pacific Ocean. When it was finished in 1971, it was the lengthiest uninterrupted highway in the world. The reality of what we had undertaken started to dawn on me when we hit the Quebec-Ontario border. I gave Ed a pat on the wheel and told him I knew he could do it. When he responded with "Fire on the Mountain," I knew he was up for the task.

ONTARIO

Facts

354,342 square miles
Home to Canada's capital, Ottawa, and its southernmost point south of Winsor in Lake Erie
Canada's largest province in terms of population
Highest point: Ishputina Ridge 2274'
Home to Polar Bear Provincial Park on Hudson Bay
Ontario borders four of the Great Lakes, and it stretches more than 1,000 miles from east to west. It is home to Toronto, Canada's biggest city.

Quick History

Ontario was a giant wilderness, home to indigenous people and fur trappers when five thousand English, loyal to the Crown, migrated there following the American Revolution in the 1770s. The US and Canada had their worst moments in Ontario during the War of 1812 when departing, defeated Americans burnt down the city of York on land that became Toronto. In the 1850s, immigration from England and Europe resulted in an English-speaking majority. Ontario was established, as was all of Canada, on July 1, 1867, when the British North American Act established borders. It is home to Dan Ackroyd and John Candy, two of our favorite funnymen.

Hockey Opines
Notable

Almost half of all Canadians who have played in the NHL are from Ontario.

All-time team: Bobby Orr, Bobby Hull, Tim Horton, Frank Mahovlich, Phil Esposito, Ken Dryden.
Toughest omissions: Milt Schmidt, King Clancy, Toe Blake, Alex Delvecchio, Ted Lindsey.

Our next game was Saturday night and we planned to watch it in Sault Ste. Marie, five hundred miles west of Ottawa. I got tired after an hour and pulled off the highway in Rockland, drove around, and parked Ed in a shopping center. So ended our first night on the road. I had Ed play some soft, sweet Emmylou Harris to relax me to sleep.

No one sleeps in when you're in the front of a car, so we were up by 6:30. Besides, the less attention from the Dudleys, the better. We had thirty minutes to Ottawa, where we would fuel up Ed with petrol and ourselves with Pop-Tarts and coffee. Dan said he felt this was a Blues Skies day, so he clicked in Dickey Betts, and we rolled on down Route 17.

Ottawa is the capital of Canada. It stands on the southern bank of the Ottawa River, which separates Ontario and Quebec. Ottawa became the capital city because on New Year's Eve, 1857, Queen Victoria said so. In her infinite wisdom, she wanted a spot far enough away from the American border to repel possible invasion and a place halfway between Kingston and Montreal. All we knew was that it was home to King Clancy of 1920s fame and current NHL stars Denis Potvin of the Islanders and John Davidson of the Rangers, who were going toe to toe in the other semifinal for the right to be called Stanley Cup runners-up.

We were munching down our Raspberry Pops when we faced our first big decision. Parry Sound, home to Bobby Orr, was not on the highway and would be a detour of over eighty miles, but since we had to do five hundred miles over two days, we decided it was worth it. About two and a half hours later, we pulled into North Bay and saw our first massive lake. Lake Nipissing was not a "Great Lake," but to us, it was. Cal said Nipissing was 337 square miles, dwarfing the giant lake of our youth: New Hampshire's Lake Winnipesaukee at sixty-nine square miles. Since we were not in a big push that day and I knew what awaited me at trip's end, I decided to go for a swim.

Dee was the one who brought me into long-distance swimming. I would watch him swim the four-mile length of Salisbury Beach, with his white bathing cap on to protect his damaged ear. I crossed Littleton's Long Lake when I was twelve and Newfound Lake at fifteen. I was on my way to a lifetime of swims and dips. By age twenty-one, I had several US rivers and lakes notched on my swim belt. I got Lake Ontario on a family trip to Niagara Falls and a few lakes in Atlantic Canada, but no other worthy Canadian body of water. This trip would provide an excellent spring training for a summer in the Bering Sea.

We parked at a beach on the outside of town, and I tiptoed down to the shore. Being April 29, there was not a big crowd at the beach. The shock of the water took my breath away, but I slowly walked in and submerged. I was going to earn my money in Bristol Bay. The scream I emitted upon coming up woke up the loons on the lake's southern side. It was bone-chilling; I went under again, then took five strokes. I came out much faster than I went in. Dan was laughing so hard he had to hold onto Ed for fear of falling down. My lips were blue, and I was shaking like Chubby Checker doing the twist, but it felt good, my first Canadian lake.

After a fast-food lunch of burgers and fries, we took Route 11 south through Trout Creek and South River and pulled into Parry Sound about 3:00 p.m. I kept no. 4 in my pack because I did not want to look like a dopey tourist. We parked Ed downtown and walked around. What a beautiful town. Parry Sound is located on the sound that bears its name and connects it to Georgian Bay, an arm of Lake Huron.

We weren't our usual outgoing selves here. It was like being in a museum. We did not want to act out of place or behave inappropriately, which we had been known to do. We didn't talk to anyone outside of a grocery store clerk who gave us directions to Memorial Rink, where Orr had skated as a kid. We walked through the doors to the rink that was a beehive of activity and stared at the ice where Coach Bucko McDonald moved a young Bobby to defense to take advantage of his incredible speed.

When Orr arrived in Boston in 1966, he far exceeded his hype. When it was all over, at age thirty, Orr had won eight Norris Trophies, three Harts, and two Stanley Cups. The only thing greater about Bobby Orr's hockey ability was his strength of character. His humble nature and integrity were beyond anything we had seen in a famous person. To us, he was unequivocally the greatest.

We had one more stop before leaving, and that was to see the house he grew up in on Great North Road. We didn't even get out of Ed; we were so overcome, and we didn't want to make any of the neighbors or his family mad at us. We drove slowly out of town for the hundred-mile drive to Sudbury, agreeing that the detour was well worth it.

We started to smell Sudbury long before we got to it, and like Dorothy said, "we're not in Parry Sound anymore." Sudbury, a city with more than 150,000, was unlike anything we had yet seen in Canada. From Cal and Milt, we knew this nickel-smelting, smoke-stacked, black-air city had produced Ed Giacomin, who played six hundred maskless games for the Rangers. Ed had recently retired, and he was a definite Hall of Famer. He was in net when the Bruins had won our last Cup in 1972. Sudbury was also home to Wayne Carlton, who was on the ice when Sanderson fed Orr that great day in May of '70.

We thought Ed would enjoy seeing the city of another famous Ed, so we drove around for fifteen minutes. What a tough place. It was no wonder why no. 1 was totally fearless. Our eyes were stinging from the smoke, and we had two hundred miles to Sault Ste. Marie, and if we wanted to be rested for game two, we had to put in some miles. Two hours later, we pulled off the road at Blind River and got cozy in Ed on the shore of Lake Huron's North Channel. It was the end of a great first day. We had each brought a book to read across Canada so we took our flashlights out and hoped the local Dudleys would not see us.

The excitement of the previous day must have really made an impact on us because we woke up after 9:00 a.m. We still had a box of pops, but before we got our coffee, I knew what had to be done. I was too nervous from the previous day to plunge at Parry Sound, but the North Channel represented my only shot at Lake Huron, so I had to go for it. I saved my dry suit and went in with my wet one, inching my way to the water's edge. I was praying for something that wouldn't make a certain body part curl up like a little turtle, but I was dead wrong. Ice-cold! It's much tougher dipping upon waking up than it is after your day has gotten going. I peeked in my suit said goodbye to my little buddy and went under. My greater shock was turning around and seeing Dan running full speed past me into the water. He started hyperventilating and flailing his arms. He submerged and gave himself a "lake bath" because, he later explained, he didn't want to emit any Sudburyian aroma in the chance that he'd meet a young lady in Sault Ste. Marie.

We hugged the channel all the way into Sault Ste. Marie and arrived at two in the Saturday afternoon sunshine. I regretted not getting a no. 7 jersey for Espo, since this was his hometown, but I put on my no. 4 and Dan his no. 16 and we went in search of a pub where we could have fun, meet people, and steal a game at the Forum.

Phil Esposito came to us at the right time in a trade with the Blackhawks. His shot was no Bobby Hull, but man, could he score goals. Phil had the Bruins goal record by far with 76. He also had seasons of 68 and 66. Espo was a character cut from a different cloth. He was a madman on and off the ice. The best story from those days was when Esposito and Wayne Cashman kidnapped Orr out of his bed at Massachusetts General Hospital to attend the Bruins year-end party at the Branding Iron.

His unmovable presence in front of the net was a fixture that drove goaltenders crazy for years. In 1979 he scored forty-two goals for the Rangers. We were worried that because of Espo's fame in Sault Ste. Marie we would only get the Ranger game, which was scheduled for the same time as the Bruins game.

We parked Ed in front of the St. Mary's River, about two hundred yards from the International Bridge that connects the two Sault Ste. Maries: the Canadian and the American. We sat on a park bench and watched thousand-foot water giants crawl past us on their journey through the locks and canals that would send them into Lake Huron. We were mesmerized by this technology. That these mammoth ships could navigate on lakes one thousand miles inland was a testament to the colossal size of the Great Lakes.

We approached a half dozen hockey-looking people and got what we were looking for. The Alpha, a bar on West Portage Ave, was our target. We walked through the door twenty minutes before puck drop and asked if they had the Bruins-Canadiens game. When the bartender said yes, we ordered two Blues, gave him a good tip, and yelled, "Go, Bruins!"

The Alpha in Sault Ste. Marie and Winston Churchill's in Montreal have nothing in common other than they both are filled with hockey nuts. This crowd was maybe fifty-fifty with several Red Wings and Ranger jerseys. Throw in some Chicago Blackhawks fans because of Phil's little brother Tony, and you get a mixture of everything hockey.

The first period was up and down with many quality shots for both teams. Donny Marcotte tried going top shelf, but Dryden was a millisecond ahead of the puck. Cheevers stopped a Larry Robinson missile from the blue line and the period ended scoreless. By now we knew most of the patrons and had our own sort of fame. Two guys going to Alaska (true), former college hockey players (bs), Bruin season ticket holders (mostly bs), and best friends with no. 17 Bobby Miller from our home town of Billerica, Massachusetts (bs and bs). When Rick Middleton beat Dryden at 7:42, our eruption of joy was contagious. I think we turned several middle-of-the-road supporters over to our side that night. When McNab scored three minutes later, we started to think swipe a W. We didn't even have to articulate it into words—just a big sigh of hope and a roll of the eyes—and we knew what the other guy was thinking.

Then *bang bang bang!* Jacques Lemaire on a power play at 17:41. Bob Gainey less than a minute and Mario Tremblay a minute after that. Three goals in two minutes. We were dumbfounded. Our new friends tried consoling us, buying us beers, telling us the Bruins could come back, but we knew it was over. Lafleur at 4:50 extinguished any hope of a possible comeback. Chartraw made the final 5-2. We were down 0-2. We exchanged hugs and handshakes with our new friends.

Provincial Park was an hour away and since I kept my Blue intake to a minimum I took the shift. I had Ed crank out Neil Young crooning about North Ontario but even down 0-2 I felt far from Helpless.

In my life I can only compare the feeling I had the next morning with the morning I woke on the South Rim of the Grand Canyon. The overwhelming feeling of awe I experienced that morning would always be number one in my life. That frosty April morning was number two. Lake Superior, or Gitche Gumee, lay in front of me, all 31,700 square miles of it. The only sounds I heard were the birds as I crawled out of Ed's front seat, standing there in total amazement at the natural beauty.

Dan is a man of many words. His mouth is always yapping, but when I turned and saw the expression on his face, I knew he felt the same. I took my time entering Superior, trying not to let the freezing water detract from the moment. I wanted to relish the significance of this dip in my third Great Lake. I took at least ten strokes before letting loose with my primal frozen scream. This time no loons on the other side were bothered because the other side was Michigan, about fifty miles away.

We took our time getting ready, soaking up the spot where we camped. Even Ed seemed to relish the view he had from his parking spot. We looked back as we pulled out thinking how lucky we were to be exposed to such a wonder. At WaWa we took a picture of Ed next to a sculpture of a giant Canadian goose, wings spread toward the lake, very impressive. We filled our bellies and headed northwest.

Route 17 went inland for the next hour, depriving us of any Superior views, but we reconnected in Marathon, and the lake was our companion for the next several hours. I never tired of looking at it.

We pulled into Thunder Bay at 6:00 p.m. on Sunday night. We had driven over 430 miles since leaving Sault Ste. Marie, all of them with Superior. We would leave the lake and head north to Winnipeg, but Superior still had two hundred miles left before its western terminus in Duluth, Minnesota.

We pulled into a parking lot on the shore next to some docks and seaworthy giants and headed off in search of a reasonable restaurant where we could plan out our strategy for game three.

"I hope there's a jukebox," Dan said as we walked into a place on Cumberland Street.

"Why?" I asked.

"Because I want to hear Gordon Lightfoot sing about the Edmund Fitzgerald. It has an entirely new meaning for me now."

We dropped down into a booth and unfolded Randy and tried to figure out the next two days. When we saw the menu and the prices, we ordered big: chili, cheeseburger plate, Sprite, and Pepsi. When our waitress saw our chaos, she asked where we were going.

"We're halfway to Alaska," Dan chimed in, his face already covered in chili.

"I'm afraid you're not," our waitress said, "not unless you're from Mexico." Annie was from Newfoundland, and she and her boyfriend had moved to Thunder Bay three years ago.

"Why did you want to leave the Rock?" I asked.

"Twenty-five percent unemployment and winters that last eight months, for starters," she said.

"Are you related to Joey Smallwood?" Dan asked seriously.

"No. How do you know so much about Newfoundland, anyway?" Annie asked.

I explained that we were geography geeks, obsessive-compulsive nerds who grew up trying to stump the other one on trivial nonsense.

"Would you hold it against me if I knew that Newfoundland has 42,031 square miles and it wasn't part of Canada until 1949 and that your top NHL goal scorer is Tony White?" I asked.

"You know hockey too. Just wait here. Don't move. Kevin, my boyfriend, has to meet you guys," she instructed us, forgetting for a second that we were not going anywhere until we paid her for our burgers and chili.

Kevin was a guy our age who worked as a longshoreman on the Thunder Bay docks, who was also a crazy Montreal Canadiens fan. When we told him our mission he asked Annie if they could have a party in our honor. "Your tip hangs in the balance!" a sarcastic Dan said, knowing full well she was up for it.

"Call Ritchie and Cathy and Billy. He spent time in Boston," Annie instructed Kevin.

We were going to a party. We settled up with Annie and gave her a $25 tip on a $25 meal, but really, how often do you go into a restaurant and leave with a party planned in your honor? Kevin followed us to Ed, and we introduced him. Then we followed Kevin to his house, four miles from town on a quiet cul-de-sac.

That night was one of the best in my life. We were US hockey ambassadors at a state function in Canada. I'd never felt more important. Right away Dan and Kevin started to get into it about who was better, Gordie Howe or Maurice Richard. In the end, they agreed to disagree. Dan, however, reluctantly accepted that in our time, no one could compare to Dryden. The last I heard them they were in an argument over who would win a fight between Stan Jonathan and John Ferguson. Dan was having the time of his life—someone on his level giving it right back to him.

I was introduced to Billy, who had played hockey for Boston College but never made the NHL, and a couple from Winsor who were big Red Wing fans. New friends have never come easier. They thought our adventure was awesome, and some dreamed out loud of hitching on with us before reality set in. At midnight Kevin told us to crash on the couch and floor, and he was only sad that it wasn't Saturday night because he had to be at the docks in seven hours. We gave him a hearty hug and told him Bruins in six. We promised to keep in touch. I won the coin flip for the couch.

The next morning Annie told us to use the shower before we hit the road and made us scrambled eggs and bacon. When we tried to tip her, she would have none of it. She wanted a refrigerator magnet with the state flag of Alaska, and we told her it was done. We gave her a hug and tried to convey the gratitude and fellowship we felt for her and Kevin and for all the Thunderites.

"No worries, eh. You just make sure you drive safe, you crazy Yankees."

We cranked Free Bird to give Annie a last memory of her new American friends.

It did not take us long to be in a wilderness that we had not yet experienced. Away from Superior, the land stretched flat and towns were farther apart. We were heading to Ontario's wild west, Kenora, on the shore of Lake of the Woods, about four hours away. Dan took Ed and I scanned through Milt seeing who had come out of Kenora. I was out in thirty minutes.

Lake of the Woods is a massive lake that touches Ontario, Manitoba, and Minnesota. It is the most northerly point of the lower forty-eight. A nub of US land called Angle Inlet is the only US land that is north of the 49N latitude, not counting Alaska. Lake of the Woods is 1,679 square miles, and it has 14,559 islands and, including these islands, over 65,000 miles in shoreline. No wonder it is a vacation paradise for the outdoor types.

Kenora is a city, but to us, it resembled a wilderness vacation outpost. A few NHLers had come out of Kenora. The best among them we thought was Gary Bergman of Red Wings fame. Randy told us that there were not many islands right off the highway, so when I saw one less than a hundred yards out, I got hit with a great idea. I figured that if I swam to that island and back, I could claim that I swam across the Lake of the Woods. My story might even be embellished to imagine that the unnamed island was actually Minnesota, conceivably swimming across international waters. I could not turn down the opportunity. I had two freshly dried suits, thanks to Annie, who insisted we do a laundry, and slid into it in the front seat.

These lakes were not aware that the calendar said May and that was supposed to mean warmer. It was bone-chilling, but my job training and outrageous claim awaited. This would be my longest swim of the trip, if you could say that about a sprint of two hundred yards. I had to swim with my head above water because the water froze my forehead.

As I stumbled on to my unnamed island, I knew I had made a terrible mistake. My legs were numb, and I started to shiver. Being a WSI, I knew this could go badly. What saved me was that May 1 was unseasonably warm, so when I stumbled on the island's shore, I did fifty jumping jacks to circulate the blood and did my best Edwin Moses impression, hurdling as much water as I could before beginning the swim back. I yelled to Dan in a semipanic to look for a rope if I couldn't make it.

The fear of drowning set my arms into a wild frenzy of motion, and I finished the swim with the grace of a thousand-pound longhorn crossing a Texas river. Dan just shook his head and handed me a towel. He had the foresight to start Ed and turn on the heat. Much appreciated, cuz.

It was a valuable learning experience. I told him that now I knew the edge of the envelope and just how close I could come to it. Come to think of it, it would probably save me from being washed ashore on some Alaskan village. He wasn't buying any of it. We turned around and drove five miles back to Kenora and got some deli, bread, and hot, hot coffee. I still had the shiver of Lake of the Woods.

We were saying goodbye to Ontario.

From Thursday night, when we left Montreal after losing game one, until Monday afternoon, we had put over 1,200 miles on our boy Eddy. Our hearts filled when we saw the sign entering Manitoba because it represented the first new place we had visited. We pulled Ed in front of the sign and took a picture. We put on Bachman Turner Overdrive, Manitoba's favorite rockers, and belted out "Takin' Care of Business."

Manitoba

Facts

213,729 square miles
Highest point Mount Baldy, 2730 feet
Land of 100,000 lakes
Borders Hudson Bay in north east
Winnipeg home to Hudson Bay Company Museum

Hockey Opines

All-time team: Tom Johnson, Bill Mosienko, Bobby Clarke, Andy Bathgate, Reggie Leech, Terry Sawchuk
Toughest omission: Dennis Hextall, Jack Streely

It appeared to us that the original mapmakers said, "Hey, it looks like the Great Plains begin right here. What do you think?"

"Looks about right to me, eh."

The change was instantaneous; one minute we were in wooded lake country, and the next minute we were on the Great Plains, flying west in Falcon Eddy, our Conestoga wagon. We saw camping signs for West Hawk Lake, so we pulled in and set our tent up for the first time. On a cool Monday, May, Manitoba night we were the only campers on the beach. Wood scrounging was easy, and we made our campfire. The flames kept us entertained for the next three hours. We were in Manitoba, and we felt great! Game three was the next night and that was a must-win. We knew Cherry was pulling Cheevers and going with Gilbert. We had a well-earned sleep.

Since I had dipped in thirty-two US states and, so far, three provinces (having done Nova Scotia and New Brunswick as a kid); I had to add Manitoba to my gun belt. I approached West Hawk the way I entered all of my Canadian lakes, that is to say a slow tiptoe. However, on this occasion, the shock wasn't the sting of the water temperature but the balmy temp of West Hawk. I didn't let on to Dan and went for twenty strokes submerged, turned around, and began treading water.

"Body is used to these polar lakes by now," I said. "Think I might push the envelope and go for the crossing."

Dan knew my BS a mile away. "What ten, fifteen degrees warmer than usual?"

"Easy," I replied, savoring the warm, clear water of West Hawk Lake.

We stopped for coffee in McMunn and eased Ed back onto 17. Ed was performing above and beyond, and we still were not halfway to Anchorage, so we told him that today would be an easy day, and he'd have a good long rest. He surged to eighty miles per hour upon hearing that news. He did have a V-8 under his hood, even if he wasn't one for showing off. We put on his tape of "Great Car Songs" and cued his favorite Hot Rod Lincoln, by Commander Cody. He got so worked up that we had to calm him down. We could not afford to have a Dudley giving us a speeding ticket.

When you drive across Kansas to Colorado, you can see the snow-covered peaks of the Rockies many miles before entering Denver. That was the only thing I can compare to the feeling I felt as I saw the skyscrapers of Winnipeg sprouting out of the Plains, like the Emerald City of Oz. Winnipeg, Canada's seventh-largest city, was west of Kansas City, Missouri, and home to the noble Bill Masterson and the Hudson Bay Company Museum.

The YMCAs across North America are the best bang for the buck, if you desire a clean bed, a hot shower, and your wallet not to say ouch. If you can conform to the YMCA rules of behavior and etiquette, you can get a room for peanuts. We pulled into the Emerald City, found the Y, and checked into a double for $26. After a hot shower, we put on our jerseys, no. 4 and no. 17, and headed off in search of Winnipeg's best sports bar. After asking five people, and getting the same answers, we headed for the Silver Heights on Portage Ave. Portage Ave was a long walk, but we wanted to let Ed sleep, so we hoofed it. When we walked through the door, we knew we had made the right choice.

"Uh-oh. Bruins fans," we heard as we headed to the bar.

"C'mon," Dan shot back. "No Johnny Peirson fans in here? We listen to him every night on Bruins Channel 38."

"I know Johnny Peirson," said a guy at the bar. "Tough son of a bitch."

Within one minute, we were welcomed in and began the give and take of hockey fans everywhere.

The Silver Heights was a museum to hockey and Blue Bomber football. We enjoyed the history lesson it provided. We asked if anyone knew Masterson, and nearly everyone at the Heights said they did. When the guys realized the depth of our knowledge, we gladly sat back and listened to stories. Everything we heard only reinforced what we already knew, that Bill Masterson was a special man and worthy of a major NHL award. Pictures of Terry Sawchuk, Bill Mosienko, Al Coulter, and Ab McDonald covered the walls.

Winnipeg was entering the NHL in October along with Quebec, Edmonton, and Hartford as part of the merger with the WHA. Judging from the crowd at the Silver Heights, we thought it was past due. Our new pals knew our predicament; a loss would effectively end our season.

Being Tuesday, Central time, it was a different experience than Saturday night in Sault Ste. Marie. Giles Gilbert was in net for us, and we were confident that he would step up. Don Cherry was taking a gamble, but in his years behind the Bruin bench, he had proven that he was a great coach. Cherry was a unique man. He played eighteen years of professional hockey but had only one game in the NHL, a playoff game for the Bruins in 1955. He had amassed over 250 points and 1,000 penalty minutes playing mostly for the Rochester Americans and Springfield Indians. Masterson adjectives describe Cherry. After retiring in 1972, he sold insurance until the game pulled him back in as a coach. He got a minor league gig; he demonstrated an ability to motivate players, win games, and endear himself to fans with a one-in-a-million personality. His press conferences were must-see TV. We knew he was the man to bring the Cup back to Boston.

The play in the first period was tight, and both teams were waiting for a bounce or a mistake, but none came until 12:19 when Stan Jonathan (no. 17) buried a pass from Brad Park, and we went up one. The Silver Heights version of no. 17 got a fiver from every Winnipegian he could, and we were able to breathe. The moment was too much for me. The beers were cold, the company was great, and the atmosphere was overwhelming. I started the process of over-serving myself.

No scoring in the second period but a great save by Gilbert on Lafleur. My thirst had not diminished, and I was beginning to feel the effects of my heavy consumption, a strict no-no for such a big game. When the third period was half over, we were starting to think shutout. Larry Robinson ended that feeling at thirteen minutes, and the entire season was in the lurch. When Brad Park beat Dryden at sixteen minutes, we lost our minds. They pulled Dryden, but Gilbert stepped up big-time. The sound of the Garden horn meant we had life.

Our new buds seemed genuinely happy for us, and we shook every hand in the Heights and added them to our Alaskan postcard list. I stumbled out of the door and began the long walk back to the Y. I chugged a huge bottle of water and took three aspirins, but when I laid down and the bed started spinning, I knew I was in trouble.

The soft comfy bed did little to ward off the self-inflicted damage I had done to my body. Where was my freezing-cold Canadian lake when I really needed it? Oh, woe is me. Dan had a good laugh when I came to the realization that Canadian beer had a higher alcohol content than American. I shuffled to Ed and fell into the passenger seat. Dan was still not satisfied in making my life miserable so he cranked Levon Helm, singing "The Weight."

"I pulled into Nazerath. I was feelin' 'bout half past dead. I just need a place where I can lay my head…" All I could do was laugh.

I deserved every bit of it. Never again was the pledge I made that morning cruising the Manitoba plains.

After about an hour, I started to come back to life. We were coming up on Manitoba's second-largest city, Brandon, home of HOF goalie Turk Broda. We had traveled 135 miles, and I was in desperate need of some junk food and a large chocolate shake, so we pulled into a Burger King and weighed our options. Flin Flon, our favorite place, was 350 miles directly north but off the direct line to Saskatoon, our next stop. There was no way we could make that detour and keep our schedule. It was an easy decision.

"We have to consider Ed," Dan said. "He has been clutch so far. If he's going up the Alcan, we have to 86 the Flin Flon plan."

"I agree, but I think it's incumbent upon us to make a proclamation that Flin Flon ranks no. 1 in all of Canada for goals scored per capita of population. Eric Nesterenko put in 250, and by the time Bobby Clarke is done, he'll have five hundred. You know he would look good in black and gold."

"Totally would have been a great Bruin."

We got back on the highway and let the sons of Manitoba BTO take us to the border. We had to be in Saskatoon by Thursday night, and we were already down an hour. We wanted to camp somewhere north of Regina that night. Seventy-five miles later, we said bye to Manitoba, leaving many memories, most of them great.

Saskatchewan

Facts

228,445 square miles
Highest point: Cypress Hills 4567'
Home to Lake Athabasca, in the far north where Mackenzie built Fort Chipewyan, which is located just across the border in present-day Alberta
Saskatchewan is home to Gordie Howe and all-time Bruin great, Eddie Shore.

Hockey Opines

All-time team: Howe, Shore, Sid Abel, Doug and Max Bentley from Delisle, Glen Hall

We pulled into Regina six hours after leaving Winnipeg, but because of my condition, we had a late start, so it was past seven. It was 157 miles to Saskatoon, and our budget said that we would be spending the night outside, so we took out Randy and looked for possible landing spots. When we turned north onto Route 11, we said goodbye to the Trans-Canada Highway. Instead of heading due west, we were now pointed northwest, our first turn for Alaska. Longer days, colder nights, and less population. It was said that 90 percent of Canada lived a hundred miles from the US border; we were about to find out firsthand. As long as we could get to a TV for game four, we didn't care.

Miles after miles after miles of flat, endless prairie and farms, where the tallest structures were the silos, were popping up on the horizon. We stopped in the town of Davidson and considered ourselves lucky that the general store was open. We loaded up on Pop-Tarts, deli, potato salad, Lorna Doones, and firewood. We knew from the land that wherever we camped, there would be no dead wood available for a campfire. On the east side of Route 11, we saw this body of water that was miles long and barely a hundred yards wide. The next ten minutes was spent scouting the shore for a place we could hide Ed. A grove of bushes a quarter of a mile away from the road would be our spot for the night.

Ed was used as a visual pick to our campfire, and we did not bother setting up the tent. The stars would be our ceiling this night. I tried the water, and it was warmer than West Hawk. I took my overdue swim, and the water was so inviting that Dan actually made a crossing of his own on a lake that had no name. We kept our fire low and talked about home and how everyone would be crazy with anticipation for game four. "The Garden will be rocking tomorrow night," I said, "It will be the place to be."

"I know it would be great to be there, but I wouldn't trade places with anyone right now. Good call on this trip, man."

"Wish I had a cold one to toast that," I responded. "Canada Dry Ginge will have to suffice."

It was inconceivable to me that we could just disappear in Canada like we had done every night we camped with Ed. Not once had we been told to move. By now we just considered that all of Canada was our campground. After a chilly night, we got back on the highway for what would be our low mileage day of the trip so far. It was a good thing. Ed needed to rest up before we headed straight north. I took out Milt to further research Saskatoon and issued another proclamation. Saskatoon and its suburbs produces the toughest sons of bitches in NHL history. In addition to Howe, you had Ed Van Impe, Keith Magnuson, and Dave Schultz. Lots of minutes in penalties there.

We got to Saskatoon at noon and set off on our scouting mission. Within an hour, we were in an elegant double room in the Hotel Patricia, an old rectangle of a building that was erected in 1912. The Patricia had a pub, which was intending to carry the game at six thirty that night. This comfortable setup set us back a total of $40, which we gladly handed over. "I'm taking a nap," I told Dan as I fell into a queen, in room 306.

"Not me," he said, taking out the family relic no. 9 Howe jersey. "I'm going to see if I can make some friends. Maybe I'll meet a hot farmer's daughter with a rockin' little sis."

"If you do, get me ASAP," I responded. "We'll go square dancing after the game. We can dream, right?"

"Hey, Gordie Howe put in hundreds wearing this jersey. Maybe I can score one!" said Dan, as he bounced out the door to the streets of Saskatoon.

At sixty-seven years old, the Patricia came out of a time long gone. It didn't look like she had had a facelift in decades, but to us, she was the Ritz. Dan came back alone when I was horizontal watching the news. "We got a good forecast out of the weather girl," I said. "That's as close as you're going to get to any farmer's daughter."

"No way," he came back, "I have several new friends. Maybe some of the ladies I met will come by the pub tonight. I know you are wearing your no. 4 tonight, but for the sake of survival, don't get into arguments about who is the greatest of all time, because in this city you'll get exactly zero votes."

Gordie Howe was the number one favorite son of Saskatoon. He was one of nine kids and his little brother, Vic, also played in the NHL. He met his wife, Colleen, in a bowling alley on the south side of town when he was seventeen, and made his NHL debut at eighteen, on a night he lit the lamp for the first of his eight hundred goals. He was a four-time Stanley Cup champ with the Detroit Red Wings and scored 103 points at the age of forty in the '67–'68 season. He retired from the Red Wings in 1971, only to resume his career with the Houston Aeros of the newly formed WHL. In '79, he was just coming off a season with the New England Whalers, when, at the age of fifty-one, he scored nineteen goals. Dan and I had been to Hartford twice in the past three years to see Howe play with his sons, Marty and Mark. His physical strength and his strength of character stood alone in Canadian sports history. As long as Dan kept his no. 9 on, we wouldn't be having any problems in Saskatoon.

TOO MANY MEN ON THE ICE

There was not a big crowd for the puck drop at the Patricia pub for a game that we desperately needed. A loss tonight meant we could get closed out in Montreal in game five. A win tonight, and we were even. We muffled our screams when Jean Ratelle struck first, set up by son of Saskatoon, Bobby Schmautz, who was enjoying an excellent season. But Pierre Mondou tied the game on a power play with a minute left in the first period off a sweet pass from LaPointe. Guy Lafleur put Montreal up 2-1 eight minutes into the second period, but Ratelle from Schmautz again tied the score five minutes later.

By now the pub had a decent crowd, and by the third, the place was mildly buzzing with excitement. The crowd was neither pro Boston nor Montreal, but as normal Canadian citizens, they were obligated to enjoy the game. When Peter McNab put the Bruins ahead with four minutes left, we knew better than to relax and a minute and a half later, Guy Lapointe validated that feeling with a laser that beat Gilbert. OT awaited us.

We were basket cases by then. I could hardly stand up, not because of my beer intake, which was light, but because I knew if Montreal scored our season would be done. We were not beating the defending champs three in a row. Our pacing ended when OT began, and it did not take long. Jean Ratelle ended the night at 3:46, evening the series. We went berserk hugging and high-fiving people we had just met an hour earlier.

We were way too jacked to even think about going back to our room to sleep, so we headed out into the crisp Saskatoon night and walked. Up and down Broadway to Clarence over the Twenty-Second St. Bridge twice. I bet we put five miles on the streets of Saskatoon. The sun would set close to 10:00 p.m., and we walked into the Patricia in twilight, roasted and toasted and ready for the 350 miles to Edmonton.

The series was tied at two; it was now a best of three. We had to win one game at the forum, and we knew it could happen. It was shaping up to be a classic. Maybe this would be the year that we got that monkey off our backs.

It was 350 miles from Saskatoon to Edmonton, and by now, that was cake for us. The Patricia treated us to a nice complimentary breakfast and we greeting Ed with full bellies and optimism about the series. Dan kept his Howe no. 9 on; he said he'd take it off when we got to Alberta. We needed some hard driving music to match our mood, so we put in some Bob Seger Live Bullet. Our only worry with that selection was holding Ed below eighty miles per hour, because when Katmandu came on, he usually gunned that V-8. Ed was as pumped up as we were.

The Saskatchewan prairie towns flew by: Langham, North Battleford, Payton, Lashburn, Marshall. At 2:00 p.m. we figured we'd stop in Lloydminster, a city that is in two provinces, and walk around. Lloydminster was home to a member of Bruins nation no. 14, Ace Bailey. Ace joined the Bruins in 1968 and was a member of the Cup teams of '70 and '72. Ace was not a great goal scorer, but he was a steady defensive forward and a class act. In '79, he was coming off a season with the Edmonton Oilers where, by all accounts, he had taken the Oilers young superstar, Wayne Gretzky, under his wing. We parked Ed on Fiftieth Avenue, the street that divides Alberta and Saskatchewan, put our Bruins jerseys on, and went out in search of some lunch and some Ace Bailey friends. The previous night's game had put us into a great mood and we were still celebrating. Lloydminster was a good place to do it.

"Feelin good boys, eh?" "Go, Bruins. Beat Habs," "Ace on the Cup," "All the way this year for you guys!" were some of the random comments we received just walking down Fiftieth. Even the restaurant that we had lunch in acknowledged our good fortune. Wearing our Bruins jerseys was a billboard. In Canada, if you are not up on what's going on in the NHL, you are missing the boat. It is so much a part of their culture. Nothing in the US compares. Maybe football in Alabama or basketball in Indiana but nothing that the entire country gets on board for. Before we returned to Ed, we walked across Fiftieth crossing into Alberta. Ed was mad that we entered Alberta before him, but we promised him that a big treat was coming his way.

ALBERTA

Facts

255,541 square miles (as big as France)
Highest point: Mount Columbia 12,293'
Alberta is where the Great Plains meet the Rocky Mountains. Alberta is the location of Fort Chipewyan in the northeast part of the province. The Fort is where Alexander Mackenzie began his trip to the Arctic Ocean in 1789 and his trip to the Pacific Ocean in 1793.

Hockey Opines

All-time Team: Johnny Bucyk, Neil Colville, Bill Gadsby, Norm Ulman, Ron Stewart, and young goalie Pete Peters (I just had a good feeling about him.)

Coming into Edmonton on Route 16 was different than the other prairie cities we had entered. Greater Edmonton was more densely populated, and traffic was heavy; it was also Friday night. Edmonton was also in the oil patch, which was booming. Downtown was busy and big. We put Ed in a lot, put our packs on, and headed out in search of the YMCA on 112th Street.

Game five was on Saturday night, so we would be in town for two days. A room at the Y for two nights set us back $46. Twenty minutes later, we were dining at the very reasonable Spaghetti Factory, two blocks from our front door. I had not had a feast like that since our going away dinner at Jacoby's in Tyngsboro. One glass of red wine and I was gassed. Apparently, all the good times of the previous twenty-four hours were catching up with me. I hit the sheets and was out cold.

Saying we slept in would be an understatement. It was 10:00 a.m. before we got going. This would be our last day of no mileage between Chelmsford and Anchorage, and we had some chores to take care of, specifically Ed. A Quick Lube on Ninety-Ninth Street was our first stop. It was Ed's version of a mani/pedi; he got an oil change, new sparks and filters, and his tires rotated. He was feeling so good. When we pulled him back on the road we took him to a car wash. Nothing was too good for our boy.

We cruised the downtown streets of Edmonton playing some Beach Boys. It was a week since Sault Ste. Marie, and we wanted to maximize the event of the coming evening, just like we had back in Ontario. It seemed like way more than a week had passed.

When we started approaching people about a spot to watch the game, we got several answers, so we decided on the Hotel Macdonald on One Hundredth Street—a giant built in 1915. It looked very elegant, but we were assured the game would be playing in the bar. The Mac, as everyone called it, overlooked the North Saskatchewan River. It was a spectacular venue for a big game.

We fell in love with Edmonton—a cascading river flowing right through downtown and beautiful parks. Puck drop in Montreal at seven would be 5:00 p.m. for us, now that we were in Mountain time, so we had to address a problem before we got back on the road on Sunday. We didn't need anything cluttering up our heads, and we had to put our focus on game five. Before we left Massachusetts, we swore that we would cross the border of the Northwest Territories. Of all our obsessions, one held a power always beyond our reach: the Arctic neighborhood of North America. We were now knocking on that door.

I had watched too much of Robert Flaherty's *Nanook of the North* documentary, filmed in 1922, about the adventures of Nanook and his Inuit family in the Canadian Arctic, so I devoured everything I could about the Arctic. Until now, the Northwest Territories only existed in the books of Mowatt, Peary, and Berton; but now it was knocking on my door. I had to set foot in the land that Amundsen conquered, the Northwest Passage that Sir John Franklin disappeared in with 145 men, where Parry was marooned in for four winters in the 1820s. I had to see it for myself; just setting foot in it would satisfy that compulsion. Fortunately, Dan understood this fixation and agreed to join me in my quest.

We had two options from Edmonton. One: Drive to Hay River, Northwest Territories, on the southern shore of Great Slave Lake. Turn around and drive hundreds of miles south to Grande Prairie, Alberta, to catch the Alcan (Alaskan Highway) in Dawson Creek, British Columbia. It would add on over three hundred miles, but I could dip in (sorry, Erie and Ontario) the fourth-largest lake in North America, plus the highway would be flat and easy. Or two: Drive up the Alcan to Watson Lake, Yukon and go north to Tungsten, Northwest Territories, instead of staying on the Alcan to Whitehorse. The detour would be less miles than option one, but the miles would be over the Logan Mountains in eastern Yukon. Upon reaching Tungsten, we would turn around and drive through Ross River back to the Alaskan Highway.

"I think we should go the Hay River route," Dan said. "The miles will be long prairie miles, easy on Ed. Randy says the Tungsten road is tough. If we're actually going to drive hundreds of miles out of the way just to put our foot on a map, let's take the easier way. Ed still has to do the Alcan."

"Okay," I agreed, but I was secretly disappointed that Dan did not want to do the Tungsten road. That road looked like the end of the world, whereas Hay River was a decent-sized city. "To Hay River it is," I said. "Now let's get to something more pressing."

I had looked around Edmonton for a reasonably priced Bruins, no. 9, Bucyk, but came up empty. I had perused lots of brand-new Oilers jerseys. We were thrilled that the NHL was expanding to Edmonton. As crazy fans, we knew that their cupboard was full. Good times were coming to Edmonton soon.

The bar at the Mac was crowded even at five, but unlike our previous nights, a majority of the people out were not there to watch the hockey game. A few Canadien jerseys, many Oilers, and one Flyers. We represented as the only visible Bruins fans.

The Blues were ice cold and we found a spot where we could watch the game and pace to have either moments of gloom or joy. The puck dropped at five, and we were hoping for a quick strike to take out those hideous, rabid fans that had packed the Forum. Maybe if Gilbert stood on his head, we could finally get a W up there.

They came out flying. They knew that the threat to their dynasty was real from this Boston team, and they came to play. Gilbert stood his ground for the first few shifts of intense pressure, but who else but no. 10. He opened the scoring at eight minutes, then scored thirty seconds later. The air was taken out of our sails. When Larry Robinson smoked a slap shot by Gilbert at nineteen minutes, we knew our night was over. The only thing we had to cheer was O'Reilly versus Risebourgh in the first of two fights between the two. It was the only W of the night for us. Gone was the wild energy of Winnipeg.

We had a very quiet night sipping our Blues in the shadows enduring a 5-1 beating. The walk back to 100th street was somber. We were down 3-2, and the next day we would begin the Alaskan Highway.

I don't know how James Cook or Magellan felt leaving the dock centuries ago, but I think I felt like they did on that Sunday morning heading west out of Edmonton. We saw them before we hit Whitecourt. In the distance, about seventy miles away, just sitting in their magnitude, was the Rocky Mountains. Every mile they grew bigger. They were both awe-inspiring and scary.

Dan was driving, and my mind was racing, so I wasn't paying attention to Randy or the road. When I saw the sign for Dawson Creek, British Columbia, it occurred to me that we were going the wrong way.

"Hey, Dudley Do Right, you did a wrong turn and missed the turn to Hay River," I said.

"No mistake," Dan responded. "I had a talk with Ed this morning about our options, and you know him. He's never one to run from a challenge. He wants Tungsten."

I leaned out of the window and let out a scream worthy of my Nipissing dip. I was hooting and yelling and pounding on Ed's dashboard, telling him how proud I was.

"You know we are heading into the abyss of TV availability," said Dan. "We have some long days, and who knows how many TVs there are north of sixty degrees. I don't think Tungsten has hockey night in Canada. We just have to hope for the best. We need two wins. I hope we see them."

BRITISH COLUMBIA

Facts

357,216 square miles stretching from the Rocky Mountains to the Pacific Ocean
Canada's third-largest province
You could fit four Great Britains in one British Columbia
Highest mountain is located near the Alaskan border: Mount Fairweather at 15,299'. The Fraser River and its spectacular canyon cut the province in two with its 850-mile length.

Dawson Creek is a city in northeastern British Columbia with a population of ten thousand. It was a city with hotels and bars and TVs, and we knew we could get the game there but we had three days before game six, and there was no way we were going to stay. In 1942, Dawson Creek was the sleepy western terminus of the Northern Alberta Railways, but in 1942, world events conspired to change Dawson Creek forever. The Japanese Army had invaded Alaska's Aleutian Islands and were occupying several of them. The US Army decided to build a road from Alaska to the end of the road in Canada so Alaska would be connected to the Lower 48. Dawson Creek in 1942 was the end of the road. Today Mile Zero of the Alaskan Highway (the Alcan) stands in the middle of downtown Dawson Creek.

We did the tourist thing and took the required photos. We made sure we got a nice one of Ed; after all, he was doing all the work on this. We gave him a pep talk about the Alcan and told him how proud we were of him.

The Alcan has been shortened and rerouted hundreds of times since it was finished less than a year after it was started. Many US soldiers paid the ultimate price during construction through the greatest wilderness in North America. In '79, it was a dirt road of over 1,500 miles.

We were about twenty miles out of Dawson Creek when we realized what we had gotten ourselves into. The Alcan was a flying rock fest of crazy inclines and declines, some with drops of five hundred feet over the edge of the road. Throw in truckers who drive like Richard Petty in a big hurry, and you have a recipe for terror, panic, and dread. In a word, it was harrowing.

Ed was averaging about fifty-five miles per hour, but he was slipping and sliding all over the dirt road that was mostly mud. Before we came to Fort Saint John, we crossed the Peace River, the river that Alexander Mackenzie took to the Pacific Ocean in 1793. This would be the only time we would intersect with our exploration obsession.

Ed pulled over after crossing the bridge, and I looked down on the beautiful river, looking the same as it did almost two hundred years ago. I wanted desperately to dip in the Peace River, but it would have been a long scramble down and back. I had to be content with throwing a rock.

We had stayed away from night driving for most of the trip and did not want to start now. Fortunately for us, at this latitude in May, the sun was up past ten at night. After a very long day, we saw a sign for Muncho Lake Provincial Park. Our day was over. Muncho Lake was a paradise. A giant mountain stood over the lake which was so crystal clear that you could see its bottom. It was magnificent, and we were going to camp there.

We had traveled over seven hundred miles on that Sunday, and we were gassed. Ed was exhausted, and he needed some rest. The first part of the Alcan was in the books. Ed pulled to a spot close to the lake, and we didn't even bother with bathing suits. No eyes were upon us. Despite losing feeling in the extremities, I savored this dip because it was in the most immaculate place in which I ever had the pleasure of swimming.

We set up camp, had a fire, and iced a six-pack in Muncho. We heard a car or a truck go by on the Alcan every once in a while, but we were more alone than we'd ever been in our lives. I slept like a tired baby.

Muncho was even more impressive the next day. We took our time packing, knowing that we'd never be back.

"Pictures won't do this place justice," Dan said. "I've been to the French Alps, and they look like Mount Monadnock compared to this place."

We drove slow leaving Muncho, looking back to capture every last ounce of splendor.

About two hours after leaving, we saw the sign: Entering The Yukon; 60 degrees North Latitude. Indescribable emotions flooded me. Dan knew the routine. We pulled Ed next to the sign, and I dug through my wallet for my favorite Robert Service poem that I always carried with me. I scrambled to the top of Ed and faced the north. I had dreamed of this moment ever since I had discovered Service.

The Men That Don't Fit In

> There's a race of men that don't fit in
> A race that can't stay still
> So they break the hearts of kith and kin
> And roam the world at will
> They range the field and they rove the flood
> And they climb the mountains crest
> Theirs is the curse of the gypsy blood
> And they don't know how to rest

The Yukon

Facts

183,163 square miles with a population around 30,000
It is home to Canada's highest mountain: Mount Logan at 19,551'.
It borders the Arctic Ocean to the north and Alaska to the west.
The Yukon River flows south to north through the entire territory,
    creating a giant watershed.

No one from the Yukon had ever played in the NHL.

    We pulled into Watson Lake, mile 635 of the Alcan, and went on our fact scavenger hunt. Watson Lake's claim to fame is the Signpost Forest, started by a homesick US GI in 1942, when he put a sign with mileage to his hometown on a tree on the side of the highway. Since that day, tens of thousands of signs have been added.
    We headed for the Watson Lake General Store for answers. Man, did we hit the motherlode. Carl was a German who had lived in Watson Lake for years. He was a walking encyclopedia of everything we needed. Carl sold us a real good map, four boxes of Pop-Tarts, bread, beer, Pepsi, deli, a rope, and two five-gallon gas cans that we could fill at the station. Carl said that we would need the extra fuel because if we were going to Tungsten, we would find no services there. Carl spread our new map on the counter and told us what we were in for.
    "We are now in mud season, so the roads will be a challenge. The road from Watson Lake to Miners Junction is sixty miles and will be in good shape. When you get to the junction, turn right going east. It's about a hundred miles to Tungsten. It is dangerous in many

ways. The road is straight enough, but the mud can swallow you up, plus a few steep parts, go slow around these turns. Trucks are a danger at any time. One can be coming from Tungsten loaded. If a truck comes up behind you, find a place to pull over to let them by. Expect nothing in Tungsten. The mine controls everything. The miners live in small houses and apartments. Some have families. There are a couple of hundred people that live there. So crazy Yanks, I wish you Godspeed and be safe."

When we asked Carl if he had ever dealt with anyone attempting to visit Tungsten as a tourist, he said at least two or three times a year. We shook Carl's hand, attempted a bad German language goodbye, filled our gas cans, got into Ed, and asked him if he was prepared for the ride of his life. His horn blast indicated he was as ready as ever.

The ride to Miners Junction was slow, but normal dirt on a highway like the Alcan. When we saw the road to Tungsten, we pulled over and said a prayer. We were now truly on a road to the end of the civilized world. It was about three in the afternoon. The sun was out, and it was the most excited I've ever been in my life.

The next two hours were surreal. We saw no trucks coming or going. The Hyland River, a gorgeous white-water beauty, was our only company the entire ride. When I saw the sign that said "Entering the Northwest Territories," I yelled for Dan to stop. As stupid as it was, I wanted to cross into this holy land of mine on foot, like Mackenzie did in 1789. By then we knew we would see no traffic, so Dan let me out, and I walked the last hundred feet of The Yukon into the Northwest Territories. A lightning bolt shiver went down my spine as I stepped over the border. The joyful feeling was like nothing I had ever experienced in my entire life.

Northwest Territories

Facts

1,322,910 square miles with less than 50,000 people
Highest point Mount Nirvana 9098'
Northwest Territories has three of the largest ten islands in the world.

Brief History

Baffin, the largest island, is fifty thousand square miles larger than Japan. Martin Frobisher in 1576 was the first European to explore and map the coast of Baffin Island. Henry Hudson got set adrift there, with his son, by his mutinous crew. In 1789, Alexander Mackenzie set out from Fort Chipewyan on Lake Athabasca in a canoe, and made it down the river that now bears his name to the Arctic Ocean. The search for the Northwest Passage took hundreds of years and hundreds of lives to solve. In 1905, when Roald Amundsen telegraphed Europe from Eagle, Alaska, to announce the successful navigation of the Northwest Passage, the age of exploration for the land that became the Northwest Territories was at its end.

No one from the Northwest Territories had ever made the NHL.

We had five miles of road before we hit the bustling metropolis of Tungsten. It was like nothing I'd ever seen. There were bunkhouses, some houses, and a school. There was a tiny post office and a store that was closed; all of it squeezed into a beautiful valley surrounded by mountains. The mine was east of town and that was for company vehicles only. This was as far as we were going. A bunch of little kids came up to us and asked if we were scientists or reporters. I felt like Neil Armstrong. Our arrival caused such a stir that in no time at all, half the town had surrounded Ed. I felt like a celebrity. Ed was beaming from all the attention.

Everywhere we had visited in Canada had welcomed us with open arms, and Tungsten was no exception. We accepted an invitation to the Chemery house. Sue was the mom of three and worked in the post office; and her husband, Mike, was a mechanic and, like everyone in Tungsten, worked for the mine. Sue invited us to dinner, but before eating, the kids wanted us to climb Mount Baldy, which one of them described as "the mountain in the backyard." We put on our bear bells like neckties, so any grizzlies could hear us coming and run the other way, and started ascending the mountain.

The posse of kids was exceptional in many ways. They could climb like mountain goats and never stopped asking us questions. What did we do for work? Why were we going to Alaska? Had we ever been to New York City? Did we have girlfriends? What was our favorite part of Canada? Why did we like hockey so much? When we managed to get a word in edgewise, it was our turn to ask the questions. Most of the kids had been in Tungsten for years, and while they dreamt of what life on the outside would be like, not one would leave Tungsten. It was a wilderness paradise to them.

They did not have TV, but they had VCRs and a healthy supply of movies that they traded around like baseball cards. They had short wave radio, and when the sun went down, they could get the AM stations out of Yellowknife, Whitehorse, and Fairbanks. These kids were knowledge magnets. They all read books, and they were interested in everything from sports to geography. They reminded us of us. I thought to myself, for the first time, standing on Mount Baldy looking down at Tungsten, I could be a teacher.

We scrambled down Baldy and had a dinner of spaghetti and meatballs, as good as the Spaghetti Factory in Edmonton. Sue told us that twice a month they would give their food order to one of the mine employees, and their groceries were delivered to their door. Mike, who was from southern British Columbia, told us the wages were very good and there was little turnover at the mine. Half of the mine workers were single men who lived at the bunkhouse, but now there were enough families in town to have a school. The school was a three-room building that taught kids from grade 1 to grade 12; two teachers lived in town during the school year. The Chemerys had been in Tungsten for five years. Once a year they would go on a vacation for two weeks, and they'd been all over North America. The kids cleared the table, and we just sat there and talked. Mike wanted to know the origin of our obsession with the North.

"My Dad was a history professor, and he loved the Klondike stories. I guess I'm a product of my upbringing," I said. "Going to the Yukon and the Northwest Territories was a dream come true, and reality has exceeded my wildest imagination."

Sue offered to drag out the extra mattress to lay out in the main room, but we told her we were comfortable in Ed; besides, tomorrow was a school day, and we didn't want to be in the way.

"It's a pleasure to have you," she replied.

Mike raised his glass of ginger ale and said, "To our visitors, the crazy Americans. We're not big hockey fans, but for your sake, we hope your Bruins win the Stanley Cup."

Leave it to Dan to respond with a toast of his own. It was right on the money, and it expressed our sincere thoughts on this incredible country that we had been guests in for just under two weeks. I had to turn away for fear of someone seeing me get emotional. When we settled down in Ed for the night, I told him that his words were well said.

"Easy, man, straight from the heart. This country is chock-full of extraordinary people."

Our first night in the Northwest Territories was freezing. I was glad I had Willie, my LL Bean sleeping bag, to keep me toasty.

The commotion of kids heading off to school was our alarm clock at 7:00 a.m. The sun had been up for hours. We said our goodbyes to these people, who were now our friends, and promised we would send the kids T-shirts from Alaska.

"Come back anytime," Sue said. "The door will always be open for a couple of road warriors."

Mike told us to be careful on the way out and hit the Gold Rush Inn in Whitehorse; it was the place to be in the big city. We shook hands and drove away right past the school; all the kids came out to wave bye to us.

Dan shook his head and said, "We could live two hundred years, and we would never experience anything like the past twenty-four hours. I'm actually sad to leave."

"Me too," I said. "That place will stay with me forever."

It was about four hundred miles to Whitehorse, and it was an entirely dirt road, so we pushed Ed going back down the Tungsten road. When we got back to the Ross River Highway, we saw a strange sight—a hitchhiker. We had picked up a few hitchhikers across Canada, but never for long rides. So here was this guy just standing there with his thumb out, literally in the middle of nowhere. I knew the sad look on his face from my years on the road. We stopped. I got out to let him in the back.

And he said, "Thanks, man. I thought I might spend the night there. Not a lot of traffic on the road today."

His name was Luke, and he was from Faro. We told him we were going to Whitehorse to watch the hockey game but we'd take him as far as Ross River, about 160 miles away.

We were on the Robert Campbell Highway and came up on a handsome lake east of the road. Frances Lake looked inviting for a dip, but we were tight for time, so I kept my thought to myself. When the subject of hockey came up with Luke, he was all over it. He was a Black Hawks fan because he liked the jerseys. He wanted a Rangers-Montreal final. He was looking forward to tonight's game but was not worried because they would have the game in Ross River if he didn't make it to Faro.

"How long have you been getting game feeds?" I asked, amazed that TV had come to a place so remote.

"We've had games in Faro for as long as I can remember. It was back in '72, when we were playing the Russians in the Canada Cup, and everyone from Ross was making the forty-five-mile ride to Faro for every game. Then this guy from Ross River got so pissed off that he rented a helicopter, strung a radio line from Whitehorse to Ross River, by helicopter, hopping the mountains. All the newspapers over the country did stories about the guy, but all he wanted to do was just listen to the games."

"Listen to the games?" I asked.

"Ya. CBC radio. No TV yet. You have to go to Whitehorse if you want to watch a game."

We were making decent time and on schedule when I saw a truck approaching, heading south. Ed already had sustained a "Yukon" windshield, which is a crack begun by a flying rock that turned into a spiderweb of cracks spreading all over. The truck kicked up a wave of dirt, rocks, wind, and mud. When a big rock struck right in my sight line, I panicked and spun the wheel so sharply that Ed skidded out and careened into a ditch. For a split second, I thought Ed would roll. In that instant, the end of the trip flashed before my eyes. When Ed came to a stop, I took a gulp and looked at my passengers. We all were okay. We got out to take a look at Ed. His fender was bent, and a tire was flat, and we were stuck in a ditch fifty miles out of Ross River, three hundred from a TV in Whitehorse. It appeared to us that game six was not going to happen.

We put Luke behind the wheel after changing the tire. Dan and I tried to push, but we could not get out of that ditch. We tried for a half hour before giving up. We would need help.

We waited and waited. An 18-wheeler flew by us without giving us a second look. Two hours later, we saw a pickup and flagged them down.

"Damn, Luke!" shouted the driver. "You got yourself stuck good!"

They were friends of Luke's, and they were returning to Faro after a vacation in Alberta. They had a chain which they wrapped around Ed's bumper, and we were out of that ditch in twenty seconds. We had to force a twenty on them for beers tonight, said goodbye, gave them Luke, and limped on down the road.

It was now three o'clock, and we were in Pacific time, so there was no way we were making Whitehorse. Luke had given us hope, and the closer we got to Ross River, the more that that hope was realized. Ed was beaten up badly and was complaining with every RPM, so we knew we had to rest there.

On his radio dial was the dulcet voice of Danny Gallivan of CBC Broadcasting. "High above a packed Boston Garden for game six of this magnificent Stanley Cup semifinal…"

We could not believe our ears. We drove to the one-stop gas station-general store in Ross River, bought a cold six-pack, then drove down the road a half mile, settled in beside the Pelly River, and got ready for Hockey Night in Canada in Ed. God bless these obsessive Canadians with their hockey.

This was our first game not on TV, and although we had grown up listening to Fred Cusick and Bob Wilson, two of the very best, it was a different experience on radio. As huge hockey fans, we couldn't see a play develop, so we had to rely on the radio announcer to do that for us. Fortunately, Gallivan was so good you could hear the inflection in his voice as scoring chances unfolded. Of all the games, this was our most bizarre setting, but we were not complaining. This game was win or go home, end of season. The season and the Cup were on the line.

Things started badly. Larry Robinson from Mondou at eight minutes, with the typical howitzer, started the scoring. Stan Jonathan, no. 17, answered two minutes later, and then the underappreciated no. 29, Donny Marcotte from Ratelle, and Schmautz put us up 2-1 at twelve minutes. We felt good for all of thirty seconds because Mondou beat Gilbert on a pass from Yvan Lambert. The period ended 2-2. We had already consumed our six, so we walked back into Ross River for another pack. We needed the walk to shake off the tension as we spent the entire first period walking back and forth and around Ed.

The second period was quiet until the sixteen-minute mark when Wayne Cashman put us up 3-2, and that was how the period ended. We knew that a one goal lead entering the third period against these champions was not comfortable, but at seven minutes, no. 17 gave us a two-goal cushion. Then he did it again. Stan Jonathan at fifteen minutes ended the suspense, notching his hat trick and sending the series back to Montreal for a game seven. Jonathan had played the game of his life at the biggest moment of his hockey career. According to Gallivan, Gilbert was brilliant, stopping twenty-five shots.

We were over the moon! Game seven! I could already feel the nerves bubbling in my gut. Since it was seven thirty and we had three hours of light and 230 miles to Whitehorse, we jumped in Ed, thanked him for letting us listen to the game, cued up some Crossroads from Clapton and his Cream buddies, and headed south for the first time on the trip.

Two hours later we pulled into the shore of Quiet Lake and voted 3-0 that the lake was appropriately named. We found plenty of dead wood, set up our tent, and had a toasty fire. It was the end of a long, stressful, frightening day, but we dozed off happy; the most displaced Bruins fans listening to Emmy Lou belt out "Easy from Now On."

Quiet Lake lived up to its name the entire night, and we slept late. We were about three hours out of Whitehorse, and we had some planning to do. It was Wednesday, May 9. Game seven was Thursday night. We had done well with our budget, so we decided to spend two nights in a Whitehorse hotel. We would watch the Bruins dispatch the Canadiens and skip into Alaska, getting to Anchorage in plenty of time for me to catch my flight to Dillingham on May 12. It would be the perfect end to the perfect trip.

Johnsons Crossings, Jakes Corner, and Marsh Lake were the suburbs of Whitehorse. Traffic wasn't much of a problem here since Jakes had a population of ten. Whitehorse was named after rapids on the Yukon River because they resembled the mane of a white horse. We were rubber-necking so much when we saw the town that we missed our exit off the Alcan. The highway circled Whitehorse from one hundred feet up so we got a great look at the city in the valley.

Whitehorse was a cozy, spotless city with hotels, restaurants, tall office buildings, and noise hugging both banks of the Yukon River, nestled in a valley with mountains on every side. It was charming. The *Guinness Book of Records* said that Whitehorse had the least amount of air pollution of any city in the world. It seemed strange being in a city after hundreds of miles of forest.

We parked downtown and went hunting for what would be base camp for the next two days. First stop was the Gold Rush Inn. It looked expensive, but we had been good with our budget, so we went all in. The Gold Rush had a great pub, but they had TVs in the rooms that carried the game. Game seven could not be watched in a pub with external noise and distractions; we needed total focus for a game of this magnitude.

Our room was magnificent. We decamped and set out on the tourist trail. Dan knew, from my many party performances of "The Cremation of Sam McGee" by Service, that I'd be dipping in Lake LaBerge. Lake LaBerge is a half hour north of Whitehorse, and a dip there would top my list of literary dips, displacing the Mississippi River and the adventures of Tom Sawyer. LaBerge was famous for not only Sam McGee but also *Call of the Wild*, the masterpiece by Jack London.

LaBerge is named for the first French Canadian to explore the area, Michael LaBerge. The lake is known as Kluk-tas-si by the First Nation Tagish people. LaBerge is really not a lake at all but a widening of the Yukon River. Some widening, it is thirty miles long and up to three miles wide.

Ed took his time on the little drive north. It was really a day off for him, and he was enjoying the tourist thing as well. He hadn't heard his car songs tape since Route 17, so we cued up some Beach Boys and jammed some Little Deuce Coupe. We had to tell Ed that we were going to the beach, but it was not in Southern California.

We found a spot on LaBerge that was meant for swimming and camping. I prepared for a shock to the system. As soon as I put my toe in I knew that this would be my biggest challenge. LaBerge was like a giant tub of ice. Muncho, until then, was my coldest plunge, but this was worse.

I thought to myself, *What am I getting myself into with this Bering Sea gig?*

I took ten strokes with my head in the water and, legit, started to lose feeling in my legs. My head was screaming like I had guzzled a Dairy Queen freeze with one gulp. I could not stand up and walk out. I had to crawl and support myself with my arms to attempt to stand in the shallow water.

I was in the process of warming up in Ed when a car with Ontario plates pulled up at the beach area and four people with bathing suits popped out. *Schadenfreude* is a German word which means getting pleasure out of someone else's misery. I was about to get some big-time schadenfreude. The two couples dashed into the lake screaming; when the reality of what they had done was apparent on their faces, I knew I had found some soul mates. One of the girls did not submerge, and I was quick to point out to her that you had to immerse your entire body if you wanted credit for the dip. To my pleasant surprise, she followed my directions.

They were two couples; one from Canada and one from New Zealand. They had left Toronto two weeks ago for a cross-country adventure and were heading back east after their visit to Whitehorse. They were peppy and funny and full of questions about our adventure. We hit it off right away. They wanted to know if we had been to Takhini Hot Springs yet. We had not, but we were happy to join up with them to explore another natural wonder.

Putting my suit back on and going for another dip was the best move I had made in four thousand miles. The Takhini Springs was a paradise of natural warm, 102 degree pools. It extinguished the bone-chilling shiver I had since my dip in LaBerge. We christened the new friends the Can-Zealanders. Martin was their troop leader, and he was from Toronto, as was his girlfriend, Sarah. Martin was a fanatical Maple Leafs fan that had a deep hatred for the Montreal Canadiens. When we told him that we had created an All-Star Team from every province, he wanted to hear the all Ontario team. He was disappointed, but not surprised, that no Maple Leafs made the cut. He was a fan of hockey, on our level, like the guys at the Silver Heights in Winnipeg. He knew the anxiety that was gripping us a day out of game seven.

The Can-Zealanders were also staying at the Gold Rush but were intending to begin their road south on Thursday morning. We made plans for dinner and shuffled into Ed when we found out that their Chevy Nova had no name. We were beside ourselves. We asked them if they could name their vehicle and park it next to Ed at the Gold Rush so he could have a friend. Forty-five minutes later, we got back to town and were introduced to Lola; she had pulled in right next to our boy. Despite his Yukon windshield, he looked like a million.

The springs had the effect of a giant sleeping pill, and I was out like I'd been hit by a Joe Frazier left hook. Two hours later, I woke up feeling like a million. The Can-Zealanders had two separate rooms that connected. We got pizza from Klondike Pizza and a case of Blues. Sarah and Emily had the night planned, and we were happy to tag along. Our first stop was the Frantic Follies, a ruckus display of everything historic Yukon. We made sure to not get caught up in the excitement and overserve. We could not wake up for game seven with heavy heads. The more time we spent with Martin, the more we realized that he was our long-lost cousin. We told them they could crash in our room the next night if they wanted to stick around for game seven. We knew that Martin was all for it, and Carter, the New Zealand guy, was up for anything. Sarah and Emily were funny, bawdy, beautiful, and very low maintenance. We would borrow a baseball term to describe them: five tool players. They were all in.

We left the Can-Zealanders at the Airport Lounge at midnight and said we'd catch up with them the next day. We got back to our room and sank into our queens. Sleep did not come easy. We were already feeling the butterflies; the excitement of the day took our minds off the pending puck drop, but now that we were less than twenty-four hours away, it started to set in.

Thursday, May 10, was a dreary day. We had been very lucky with weather on the crossing, but that day was cold windy and raw. We met our friends for a late breakfast, but so consumed by anxiety as we were, we hardly ate anything at all. Martin completely understood. Since we were three hours behind, the Montreal puck was dropping for us at 4:00 p.m.

The guys headed for room 216, and the girls went shopping. Martin bought some beer, but we did not anticipate having more than one or two. Overserving can impact our enjoyment of the game.

We had two chairs in our room which Dan and I sat on the edge of and Martin and Carter used the floor. The world's two best anthems and the moment had arrived: time to drop the puck. The players were as tight as we were. Carter was new to hockey but had caught our fever. He said he loved to watch our body language as play developed and scoring chances unfolded.

All of our pent-up nerves and tension came exploding out in a deafening roar of "Yes!" when Rick Middleton lit the lamp at ten minutes. "Good start. Good start," we assured ourselves. "We need that second goal now to take out this crowd. The dynasty ends tonight!" stated Dan.

Not to be. Bobby Miller got called for hooking his second penalty of the period at thirteen minutes and Jacques Lemaire tied the game at one minute into the power play.

"What's this bs, picking on the American kid, huh?" We didn't bs Martin saying Miller was our friend. We told him that we had watched him all through high school, which was the truth. Between periods, we walked up and down the halls, and we went outside and saw that the day was clearing, then hustled back in for period two.

The second period started great for us; right off the face when Cashman from Middleton and Ratelle put us 2-1 at twenty-seven seconds. Then Cashman from Ratelle and Middleton at 16:12. We were up two goals when the horn sounded. Twenty minutes to go and a two goal lead; it could happen. If so, it would be the greatest win since May 10, 1970, exactly nine years to the day. It was destined to happen. With all due respect to the New York Rangers, who had already dispatched the Islanders in the other semifinal, this game was going to decide the Stanley Cup and everyone outside of New York knew it. These two teams were the best in hockey.

Right from puck drop in the third, the Canadiens were flying. They were pouring shots on Gilbert, and he was standing on his head for the challenge. Then at six minutes they struck. Mark Napier beat him on his glove side. Dick Redmond got called for a hook and soon after he went into the box. Guy LaPointe, set up by Lafleur and Gainey, tied the game at three. The hope and the anticipation of joy between the periods were gone. We had seen this movie before. We needed a miracle in a place where we had never gotten one.

Rick Middleton is such a fast skater that if he gets a pass at full speed, he's unstoppable. Jean Ratelle gave him that pass and at 16:01. Middleton gave us that miracle. We were up in game seven in the Forum with four minutes to go. After my outburst of joy, I had to sit down. My legs could not hold me up.

The next four minutes were a blur. I can only imagine what our new friend Carter thought. The Canadiens were raining shots on Gilbert and he was repelling every one. Then a whistle in the middle of play at 17:26. John D'Amico, the linesman, was calling a penalty on the Bruins for too many men on the ice.

"Are you god-damned kidding me! Oh my god! Are you serious?" was all I could muster.

The Bruins were changing lines. How can a linesman make that call when the Stanley Cup is on the line? We had been getting hosed in the Forum for years, but this was beyond the pale. Too many men on the ice, my ass!

The penalty kill was great. Seconds seemed like minutes. Every clear we caught our breath, if only for five seconds. They killed it for over a minute and a half, but there he was, no. 10, on the right wing. We saw it happen before it happened. Jacques Lemaire fed Lafleur over the blue line. He raised his stick for that powerful slap shot and the laser beam that came off his tape. I saw it a hundred times, but this time was different. The puck was traveling one hundred miles per hour, but I saw it in slow motion. One half inch down and it would have been in Gilbert's glove, one half inch up and it would have rattled of the post. But it was perfect. Tie game at 18:46.

We just had to regroup and get through the final minute and settle down. In overtime, who knows what might happen. The bounce of the puck makes hockey a wildly unpredictable game. Just get to OT. It was not easy; we even had a scoring chance, but the horn sounded.

We were puddles. It felt like I had no bones in my entire body. I was a giant sad mass of jelly. These emotions are what happens when you invest your heart and soul in a team for so many years as we had. If you are a fanatic, it may not be rational but it feels real. The highs are memorable and so are the lows. It makes no sense, but you can't turn it off and on. It is who you are.

The girls returned from their shopping and asked how the game was going. Dan and I just rolled our eyes and shook our heads. I think I mumbled something about too many men on the ice.

The pace at which the OT started led us to believe that the game would not go to a second OT. The puck was darting up and down the ice at a breakneck pace. Black jerseys, white jerseys just waiting for a bounce or an opening. We were on edge. At nine minutes, Middleton skated down the right wing and was one-on-one with Serge Savard. One little nifty move would put him alone in front of Dryden. But when Middleton tried to curl the puck to himself, Savard broke him up and shot the puck up the ice on the right wing where a flying Mario Tremblay gathered it in. Al Sims did a nice job keeping Tremblay from penetrating, but at the goal line, Sims could not stop the pass he sent to a streaking Yvon Lambert. The pass was tape to tape, and Lambert got it on the doorstep. Brad Park, who had played a great game, could not deflect it away, and Lambert put it in the back of the net.

Over.

We could not move. We didn't even yell. We watched the Canadiens pile over the boards and mob Lambert. We heard Bill Hewitt say, "The Boston Bruins can hold their heads high in one of the greatest series in NHL history." That was little consolation. We felt physically and emotionally empty.

"Wow," uttered Martin. "I've had some tough times over the years with my Leafs, but that…what just happened. I've never seen anything like it. Man, that was hard. Are you guys gonna be okay?"

"Ya, we'll be fine," Dan muttered, rising up to stretch, "but we're not staying here tonight. The room is all yours. We're going to Alaska."

I was glad Dan made that call. I would not have slept a minute the entire night. We needed to move. We packed our things and hugged our new friends, especially Martin. We felt as if we had known him all of our lives, even though it had only been two days. We told him that we were honored that he could share our pain. We gave the girls a peck on the cheek and said we'd keep in touch. We walked to Ed in silence.

It was only 7:00 p.m., and we had hours left of daylight. We hopped in Ed and started him up. Some Blues were in order, so we let the Allman Brothers sing our pain. Some Whipping Post and Statesboro Blues put us back on the Alcan.

The road to Haines Junction was the most spectacular we had ever encountered, but it did not register. We were numb.

A half hour later, we came to Kluane Lake. It was as if Canada was saying to us, "Don't leave yet. We saved the best for last. Stay one more night. I'll make it better."

"Let's find a spot to camp tonight," I said. "Too much is in my head. I need some time to decompress after that. I have to put this trip into perspective. We can't leave Canada like this. We have time."

Twenty minutes later, we pulled into Destruction Bay, right on the lake, which still had some ice flows.

"Don't go on that," Dan warned. "One man will be too much on that ice."

We set up camp and made our fire. We had a few cold ones that we had bought in Haines Junction. Sitting there, we recalled the past two weeks and agreed that they were easily the best two weeks of our lives. We recounted the new friends we made in Thunder Bay and in Winnipeg and Martin; the highs we experienced walking around Saskatoon for hours after game four, and the lows of Winston Churchill's and Sault Ste. Marie and Whitehorse. The unexpected joy of Tungsten and getting the radio feed in Ross River for game six was another wonderful memory.

"We have been on a four-thousand-mile roller coaster," said Dan. "I just thought it would end differently."

"Me too," I said, throwing some wood on the fire. "It's overwhelming, what we've done. This trip cannot be topped. We have set the bar out of reach."

Dan gazed into the fire and took a gulp of his beer. "You know," he said, "I am pretty sure Dryden is retiring. There is no way that they can win a fifth straight Stanley Cup. I think next year is our year."

About the Author

Steve O'Connor grew up in Chelmsford, Massachusetts, as a fanatical Bruins fan. In his younger years, he was a lifeguard at Salisbury Beach, ran track, and played college basketball. He crisscrossed the country a number of times and had many jobs before becoming an educator—a failed stuntman, oilfield roughneck, longshoreman, Inuit swimming instructor, and furniture mover, just to name a few. He became a history teacher, basketball coach, a husband, father of three children (Curran, Riley, and Flannery), and a middle school assistant principal. His love of sports and random road trips supply him with many interesting stories to share. Currently, he resides in Amesbury, Massachusetts, where he coaches track, writes, and commutes to his social studies teaching position in New Hampshire.